THE CAT COMPETITION

West Dean Summer Fête
1935

By

Luke McEwen

Published by Unchained Pen Ltd

ⱷ

Forum House, Stirling Road, Chichester
PO19 7DN, United Kingdom

A CIP catalogue record for this book is available
from the British Library.

ISBN: 978-1-910304-04-4

CONTENTS

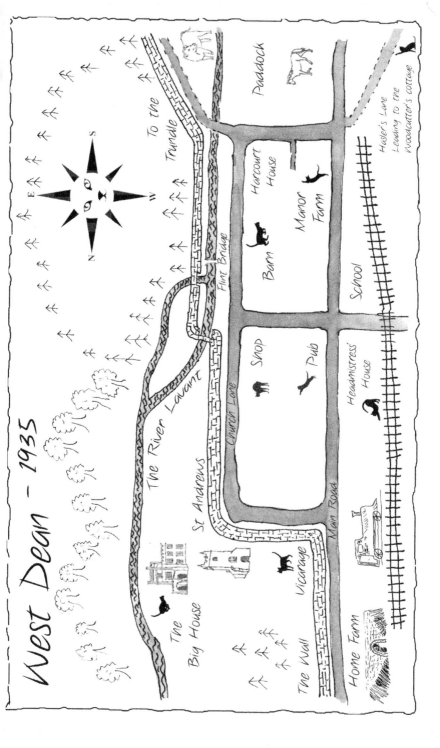

West Dean – A Place to Call Home

My name is Luke and I am going to take you to West Dean, a real village tucked away on the South Downs in Sussex. You'll hear stories about cats living with their families in the 1930s – which is a long time ago – but before I do that, I want to show you why this place is so special to me. If you're a curious cat and want to hear the stories straight away, then turn to the chapter called 'The Woodcutter's Cat' that begins on page 13. I'll still be here when you come back.

*

In 1972, when I was seven and my brother Seb was eight, we went to live with our granny for a while. We flew across the Atlantic all the way from the United States of America to England in a gigantic jumbo jet.

Mum waved us goodbye at the airport in New York, and we were entrusted to the senior flight attendant. She looked after us during the 10-hour flight with food, comics and pillows. I wasn't worried about leaving Mum and Dad as my brother was in control and I had my teddy bear, so I was prepared for anything.

Granny Rosemary met us at the airport near London. We had met her before, but because I'd left for America when I was four I didn't remember her at all. She was a lovely lady whose eyes almost closed when she smiled. She treated us as the flight attendant had: as if we were important and needed protecting.

When we arrived at her home in West Dean, Harcourt House, we were very tired but were so excited that we had to explore straight away. Everything was so different from what we were used to in America. Her house was five hundred years old and we'd come from a town where the oldest building was less than 50 years old.

Seb and I rushed from room to room, amazed at the antiques, oil paintings, wooden beams and leaded windows. When we were standing next to a mirror taller than my father and covered in gold, Granny told us that we were in the drawing room. We imagined people making polite conversation and wearing posh dresses and suits. The dining room had an enormous table that you could sit 15 people around. Granny said that it was just like King Arthur's round table. The fireplace was big enough to stand up in, and halfway up the chimney there was a priest's hole where people used to hide.

We were only going to stay with Granny for a few months but that meant we had to go to the local school, which was awkward because I had a strong American accent. I was so nervous I hid underneath my spiderman mask, keeping it on all day until Mr

3

White, my teacher, said I'd be more comfortable with it off. Suddenly my skin was bare to the winter's air and a hundred strangers' eyes were looking at me, the boy from America.

Sports at school were difficult, as I was playing by American rules. When we played football I didn't understand why everyone laughed when I caught the ball in my hands. In rounders, the bat was half the size of the baseball bat I was used to, and I didn't get a mitt to catch the ball with. Everything was just so different.

Mr White was a very kind man, though. He was a very patient teacher, and he made me feel welcome. In Chapter 4 we'll meet a very kind headmistress at the village school. She has a ginger-brown cat called Felicity, and she takes care of Felicity as well as she cares for her students.

Opposite the school is the village pub, The Selsey Arms. My Granny never went there but we would see lots of people sitting in its garden. There was a cat there who would walk between the tables, making friends and being fed. That sounds like a mighty fine life for a cat, doesn't it?

Just down the road from the pub was the village shop. Granny made our days fun by giving us 5p a day to buy sweets, which was a lot of money then. Seb and I would walk to the shop on our own and the shopkeeper would give us a paper bag to put our sweets in. He was a lovely man and always seemed to be working.

Each Sunday we would walk to church and I would

sing in the choir. It is a very small church, but there is a large organ and a tower with bells. The vicar was a friend of the family, and he would often come to Granny's house for tea, which was fun because he was a jolly man.

In the barn next door to Granny's house there was a huge haystack where Seb and I would rearrange the bales to make camps and tunnels to crawl through. It shared the farmyard with its cats. Some of them didn't seem to have a home, a name or an owner, but they managed okay. Cats who live in barns quickly learn to be self-reliant and resourceful.

Granny had two pets of her own. She had a corgi dog called Tigger, but he was not the Tigger I knew from my *Winnie the Pooh* books. He was grumpy and couldn't jump over a matchstick. Granny also had a cat called Pepper who'd sit on her lap and be cuddled like a baby. Granny would joke that Pepper, being completely black, would make a fine witch's cat.

So now you know why we're in West Dean meeting cats, but you may be asking, 'Why are the stories set in the 1930s?' Well, that was the time of my granny's childhood, and she told me a few stories I think you'd like to hear. There are people you'll be glad you met and many cats you won't forget!

Maybe living with Granny Rosemary was a bit like living in the 1930s because she liked the old ways and her house was full of antiques. This is her house in the picture on the next page.

Can you imagine if you had been born in the 1930s? There was no internet, no computers and no mobile phones. You'd travel by horse and carriage, bus or steam train. People sent letters, not emails.

Have you ever received a letter? Have you ever sent one?

In the 1930s no one had a television; instead they listened to the radio. You would help your mum with washing the crockery in the sink, and you'd wash your clothes by hand too – there were no machines for those things. You might help Dad in the garden growing the vegetables or help Mum make your own clothes. Very few people had ever flown on a plane, and many people never went on a holiday at all.

My grandmother did have a telephone, which was quite rare at the time, and because the village was so small her number was small too. Singleton two-four-five, that's all there was to remember.

And – you'll never guess – what do you think they did in houses with no upstairs toilet? Well, they kept a pot under the bed to go to the loo in!

The highlight of West Dean – I've been dying to tell you – is its Big House, West Dean Park. It looks like a castle but is really a stately home. The rooms are huge and decorated to make important people feel at home, with polished marble, huge tapestries and carved oak panels. It was the house of a very rich family who threw society parties and invited the king to stay with all his courtiers, lords and barons.

A long, tall flint wall runs right through West Dean, separating the Big House and its aristocrats from the farms, shop, pub and school and, of course, the villagers. So, life was very different depending on which side of the wall you lived on.

One day a man who had spent his childhood growing up in the Big House inherited all of West Dean, including all its land, houses, farms, forests and rivers, and the Big House too. His name was Edward James. Now, you would think that having such a fortune would make you happy, but it was not so for Edward. The woman he married was not happy with him, and when they separated he lost nearly all his friends and felt very lonely in his big, empty house. So Edward moved away, looking for happiness, and he found it in Mexico. Thirty years later, in the year I was born, he decided to give West Dean Park away and turned the Big House into a college for artists and artisans. He gave away the keys to his castle.

When I was nine, Edward visited to see how the college was faring. He was quite old by then and was a very different man to the person he was in the 1930s. He didn't mix with aristocrats any more. He'd become a poet, a sculptor and a builder of dreams. In Mexico he designed and built a surrealist garden in the jungle, filling it with huge concrete sculptures that looked like buildings from a fairy tale. You can still go there today; the garden is called Las Pozas.

Edward threw a huge party at the Big House and invited the whole village. There was a large silver screen showing a film of his magical buildings in Mexico. I remember it was a warm night, and my brother and I raced about exploring the house and its gardens. It felt so special to be there, especially since it was past our bedtime! We discovered a fishpond with a sign saying it had no bottom and was as deep as the ocean, and we also saw a big pile of earth with a sign saying it was a dragon's grave. Nearby there was a huge tree trunk made of plastic. The river wound its way through the garden and split in different ways, making a maze of waterways. A lovely place to get lost in. Strange bridges crossed the river, one made from massive pieces of flint, stuck up on their ends. After exploring all of these fantastical sights it was difficult to sleep that night, and I think it was that night when I fell in love with the village, the Big House and its wonderful garden. The village was like a little nest – a safe place in which to grow.

Now you know why I am so keen
For you to see the beauty of West Dean.
But why meet cats? Ah, that's the key!
For they're my favourite pet, you see.
Not everyone loves cats, so be on your guard
Against cat-haters – such views should be barred!
If they hear these stories and meet a few,
If they hear the wonderful things they do,
Marmalade, black, ginger or blue,
Maybe they will have a favourite too.

People say cats have nine lives, which is just a bit of fun, but the thing about cats is they do lead a double life all the time.

One minute they're curled up cuties purring for a stroke or a tickle, meowing for a morsel, but then in a moment they're ready for hunting. Their claws are out and they're crouching down to pounce. When they're in this mood, don't try tickling their tummies!

The thing you really need to know about cats is, well… they're a bit like you and me. They get hungry and they like to sleep. They don't like to be too hot but they don't like to be too cold either. Sometimes they like company and sometimes they want to be on their own.

And, just as people can be very different compared to one another, so can cats. Some prefer to be indoors, some like to be roaming the countryside, some like fish and some like chicken. There are cats that will spend all day with their owners and cats that just see their owners once or twice a day (usually at meal times). So, knowing one cat doesn't mean you'll understand another. Now, you are quite young and you might not know this yet, but it's good to meet many different sorts, and then you can work out which sort you like best. I'm going to take you around West Dean and introduce you to all of its cats, and you can see which cat is your favourite.

Now you know the Who, What, Where, When and

Why of this book you'll enjoy the stories so much more. So, then, shall we get in the mood? Look at the map of West Dean at the beginning of this book and imagine you're there. Think of cows mooing in the meadows, the old buildings with brown beams and the river sparkling as it flows through the village. The sun is shining. What a lovely day for a walk.

The Woodcutter's Cat

Let's go and see the Woodcutter and his cat. We have a bit of a walk – they are at the edge of the village, but it's worth it. We'll hear how they once were strangers but then became close. This is a story of love, and when you hear it you'll understand why a cat is often considered part of the family.

Are you ready? We'll head due south as if we're going to the sea. When we reach the railway tunnel we join Hasler's Lane. On our left is a pasture for the lamb and on our right is thick woodland. After a

13

dogleg turn at Whiteland Copse, we'll find Old Shep's abandoned hut sitting on its rusty cartwheels. Just a bit further to the other side of the chalky lane, then cross the deep ruts, and there is the Woodcutter's cottage, in among the birch and elm trees.

At one time the tabby cat lived there alone. Her dark brown, striped fur helped her disappear into the woods when she hunted for her supper. She liked to be outside and was content to be on her own all night as she searched for food and explored. She was not a house cat but preferred to be in her playground: the woods, slinking and prowling through the hazel and the oak, and finding its hidden places, old badger setts and fallen trunks. She loved to be up high in a tall horse chestnut; from there she could see the woodland floor. To her, the cottage was just a safe place for sleeping in. She rarely went to the village because she didn't like being around the busy people and their noisy ways.

One day the Woodcutter arrived with his dog and made the cottage his home too. The cat didn't like the dog but it was comforting to have the man there. He was calm and quiet.

The tabby cat didn't go to the cottage for meals; instead, the Woodcutter wanted her to hunt for her own food. That was her job.

The Woodcutter described her as the 'wild thing', but that wasn't her name. She didn't have a name. He called her 'Cat'. Sometimes it was 'Hey, Cat' or 'Oi, Cat.'

The Woodcutter and Cat got on quite well, as long as he didn't make too much fuss of her. She would say hello by rubbing up against his legs, first one side and then the other. But she didn't like to be stroked. In the evening they would share the fire. He would sit on the left and she would lie on the right.

Once he tried to see if she'd sit on his lap. He picked her up and gently settled her down. But after a polite pause she jumped off and went back to her side. They'd sit and listen to the fire, the damp wood hissing and the dry logs roaring.

When the fire sparked and let out a crack, Cat would spring up, startled, and the Woodcutter would laugh at her for being so nervous. They would stay by the fire for hours, until he went up to bed and she went out hunting. In the morning as she curled up to sleep, he was waking up and going to work.

Sometimes, on the coldest of wintry days, the dog would come in too, but Cat made sure it kept to the Woodcutter's side of the fire. She thought the dog was silly and weak. All it did was obey commands, and it yelped and barked and jumped and ran around in circles until it panted and rolled about. A very strange beast!

16

The Woodcutter removed a pane of glass from the coal chute window so Cat could get in and out of the cottage whenever she pleased. The chute wasn't dirty as he only kept wood there. The tabby cat found it much easier than having to meow for him to open the door each time.

*

The tabby's nearest neighbour was the Barn Cat. He lived near the Manor House on the farm. She'd met the Barn Cat one evening that summer. They were chasing the same rat, and when they discovered each other they stopped hunting and chased each other instead. The Barn Cat showed her the bales of hay piled high and the milk parlour that smelled creamy one minute and then of chemicals the next. The Barn Cat liked to play, and when they came across the white Manor Cat sleeping in the orchard he was naughty and jumped on top of the Manor Cat to wake her up. She was very annoyed and hissed at him.

The tabby cat became plump by the end of the summer. Not by eating too much, but from the kittens growing in her tummy. This was from spending the evening with the Barn Cat.

She tried to explain to the Woodcutter that the kittens were on the way by meowing a lot, but it was difficult to make herself understood.

Then one day the Woodcutter said, 'You're turning into a fat cat – that's not like you! I reckon you've got a litter on the way.'

Two weeks before the kittens came, the tabby pulled a coat behind the sofa and made a little nest. The Woodcutter added a cardboard box with a blanket and she spent her days there, sleeping.

The kittens came at Halloween. The cat felt it begin late in the evening. The Woodcutter kept the fire going all night, and he took the dog to the shepherd's hut so it was quieter in the cottage. He put out some water and opened a tin of Cat's favourite food. She laid down in her box and gave birth to her kittens.

When the fourth kitten came out, the tabby cat thought her work was done, but then another came, and another. In the end there were eight, and that's a big litter for a cat. There were too many – how would she feed them all? It took the whole night for them all to be born, about one every hour. The Woodcutter kept on feeding the fire, and every time a kitten was born he'd say, 'Well done, Cat!'

By the time the sixth had arrived, Cat was exhausted. She gave a faint meow to the Woodcutter, so he helped by cleaning the kittens with a warm, wet cloth. The last one was tiny and totally black. It was hardly moving, so the Woodcutter put the kitten on Cat's teat so that it could feed.

Over the next couple of months the kittens grew until they were over 10 times bigger than they were at birth. That meant they had to suckle lots of milk from Cat's tummy, and because there were so many of them she became very tired. Each day the Woodcutter kept the fire going, and during those months he opened many tins of food. Cat had one half in the morning before the Woodcutter went out and the other half when he came back. To the smallest kitten, who'd come last, he gave extra milk from a tiny bottle with a rubber top. He did that twice a day, holding the bottle in his hand while it suckled and would say, 'Drink up, Midnight.'

All the kittens together made quite a noise; they purred as they suckled the milk from their mummy's tummy and then they'd play. Cat would sometimes play with them, but more often she needed to rest.

When the kittens were big enough, the Woodcutter said to Cat, 'I've found homes for our kittens in the village, but we're going to keep Midnight.' He tickled Cat under the chin. 'And because Midnight's got a name, you should have one too. Can I call you Spark?'

In midwinter, when it was dark in the morning and dark in the early afternoon, the puddles froze and the ground was white with snow. The Woodcutter had delivered the last of the kittens to their new homes in the village, so it was just Spark and Midnight who joined the Woodcutter by the fire. Midnight sat on the Woodcutter's lap. He thought of him as Daddy.

Things started to go wrong when the Woodcutter sneezed and wiped a finger under his nose. The Woodcutter didn't go out that day; he stayed in his bed. And the next day, when he should have been at work, he never appeared. Spark watched the door at the bottom of the stairs, but it didn't open and she was worried for the Woodcutter. On the fourth day she saw the Woodcutter come down the stairs, but he didn't look like himself. He moved like a wounded fox and breathed like an old horse. All he did was go to the kitchen and open a can of food for Spark and Midnight, and another for the dog. Spark saw him cut some bread, but he didn't eat it. He just sighed and went back to bed. She knew something was really wrong, but what could she do?

Spark left the cottage, picking her way through the ice and snow, and went down the lane to the big road by Pheasant Cottages. She sat there and waited, and when she saw Ben Dunk – the boy from Home Farm – on his bike, she walked out into the road.

Ben had to brake hard to avoid Spark.

'Cat! What are you doing down here?' He reached down to stroke her but she didn't want that. 'You can't stay here in the road, you know that!'

So he stood there and looked at her while she looked at him.

'Well go on then, off you go. You'll get run over!'

Spark looked up, stepped forward and patted Ben's shoe. He put his bike down and went to stroke her, but she jumped away.

'What's up with you? You don't seem yourself!' Ben stared, trying to solve the mystery. He was about to give up and reached for his bike.

Spark saw that Ben was going to pick up his bike so she sprang onto it and sat on top of the seat as it lay on the ground.

'What!' Ben scratched his head. 'Are you after a lift home? Well, I guess it's a long walk for you – almost a mile!' He chuckled to himself, surprised that he felt so soft-hearted. 'Well, okay then.'

He picked up Spark and put her in the bike's basket. 'You do know my mum wants me home soon, don't you, and I don't want to miss my tea!'

Ben cycled with Spark back to the Woodcutter's cottage. On arrival he tried to lift her out of the basket but she just sat there and patted his hand away.

'Out you get, Cat!'

Spark lifted her paw onto Ben's hand as he held the handlebars, but when he tried to stroke her she ducked her head away.

'Well, I never!' he said, taking off his cap and scratching his head. 'What are you trying to say?'

Puzzled by the cat's behaviour, Ben got off his bike

and pushed it, with Spark still in the basket, up to the front door. He looked around. He knocked on the door, but no one came. He knocked again, much harder, and waited.

'Mr Boxall!' he called. 'MR BOXALL!'

An upstairs window yawned open and the Woodcutter croaked, 'Ben! I'm not too good, I'm afraid. Could you get your parents to call the doctor, please?'

*

The Woodcutter didn't work for a while. It took time for the colour to return to his cheeks. When he had finally recovered, he, Spark and Midnight all sat around the fire together. Because it was icy, the dog was there too.

In the beginning, Spark hadn't been sure about the Woodcutter moving in. It had seemed strange to share the cottage, but now that it's the four of them she feels as if this is the way it's supposed to be. She's still unsure about the dog – why must it bark? – but it feels nice to be part of a family, to have her son to play with, and she likes the familiar routine of the Woodcutter coming and going. And, of course, when the ground is frozen and hunting is difficult it's nice to have him there to open a tin of something tasty.

Mabel the Manor Cat

Now that we know the Woodcutter recovered from his illness, let us leave them up on the hill and go into the village itself. We can meet Mabel, a very different cat altogether! This is a story about territory, which is difficult to understand when you're small, but if you're a cat it is very important. You DO NOT WANT another cat in your territory – the space which is yours!

It's downhill all the way from the Woodcutter's home to Manor Farm, so it's an easy walk. And if Spark can do it, so can you. Be careful as we cross the main road! Now we're in Church Lane, which divides the paddocks, and on our left is the long drive to Manor Farm.

Smell the yard with the noisy cowherd, horses and pigs, but look out for that tractor! It's very busy here, with lots of men tending the fields of turnips, swedes and barley. There's so much to do.

Mr and Mrs Cooper live in the Manor House behind a flint wall with a tidy lawn and pretty flower beds. Their cat is called Mabel. She is white and fluffy and has a bit of a tummy.

Mabel has a bath every so often and can't abide mud or the farmyard pong, so she stays indoors most of the time, unless she needs to go to the loo. She will, however, inspect the front garden once or twice each day. It's quite an ordeal being outside because there is the awful smell of the farm and the annoying cat who lives in the barn. He is very dirty, and she suspects he may have fleas and not wash at all. There was an awful event in the summer when Mabel had ventured out of the walled garden to snooze in the orchard. From nowhere, the unpleasant cat jumped on top of her and then ran off!

Mabel usually starts her day in the breakfast parlour where Mr and Mrs Cooper sit reading the papers. She'll often get a bit of bacon or sausage, if she's looking pretty. Then she'll sleep in the drawing room for the rest of the morning; the windows face southeast, and she can soak up the warmth of the sun.

At lunchtime Mr Cooper comes in from the fields and relaxes with Mrs Cooper in the kitchen. He won't go into the rest of the house, so he doesn't have to take off his boots. Mabel will sit up on the stool next to the stove, as the stone floor can be rather chilly. She'll sometimes get a piece of ham or cheese from Mr Cooper's fingers.

In the afternoon, after her once-around-the-garden tour, she'll look at the pretty birds and the butterflies and dream of catching one someday. There's a sunny spot by the porch, out of the wind and just behind the plum tree, where she can spread out and unwind from the pressures of the day. She'll sit there until Mr Cooper comes back for a mug of tea and freshly baked bread at 4 o'clock. He'll sit on the porch bench where the rose bush climbs up to the roof. Mrs Cooper will bring her knitting, and they'll chat about what needs to be done on the farm. Mabel has a lick of jam from his finger and a lap of milk from his saucer.

She makes one final round of the garden, and may even risk the walled garden to sit by the pond and admire the koi. She could tell you about the time when she nearly caught one in her younger days. As the sun sets it's time to return inside, and she'll find her spot back in the kitchen while supper is being made. If she weaves in between Mrs Cooper's legs she may get a little titbit, but if Mrs Cooper is clanging and banging with pots and pans she'll disappear upstairs to the airing cupboard, which is cosy and warm.

Mabel likes to join Mr and Mrs Cooper for supper in the dining room. There is a cushion on the sofa – her favourite spot – that's not too far away from Mr Cooper in case he has a little bit of beef or salmon for her to taste.

Mabel's favourite time of day is when Mr and Mrs Cooper retire to the sitting room. Once they've lit the fire and settled down to talk or listen to the radio, Mrs Cooper will get her knitting out again, and Mabel will sit by Mr Cooper's feet until he's ready to pick her up and put her on his lap.

When they're ready to sleep, Mabel will be carried upstairs, and she'll find her spot at the end of the bed. Mr Cooper snores a bit, but she doesn't mind – it's nice to know he's there.

*

Just before Christmas it snowed horribly.

It was too cold to go outside, so Mrs Cooper put down a litter tray for Mabel to use as a loo. It was impossible to keep warm, so Mabel spent many hours sitting in the airing cupboard.

On Christmas Eve the Manor House had visitors: Mr and Mrs Magginery from London. They were staying in the Green Room for the weekend, but they arrived with enough luggage for several weeks. As

Mabel inspected the luggage she had a nasty surprise
– one of the cases was wobbling. Then her horror
grew as it made a noise. She had a sniff and knew
there would be trouble. Mr Magginery appeared and
bent down to open the case, and out popped a cat!

It was a small, but handsome, tortoiseshell. Mabel
was pleased that at least the cat was smaller than
herself, but it was so cheeky – it tried to smell her!

The cat was called Lucky. He was young and ran
around the room like a balloon releasing its air. He
played with peoples' shoelaces, got under their feet,

and performed acrobatic jumps from the stairs and mantelpiece. He even sat on Mr Cooper's lap, on Mabel's stool in the kitchen and then on her cushion on the sofa. It was as if Lucky knew exactly where she liked to sit. Then he drank from her water bowl and used her litter tray, even though he'd just been running about outside. Mabel was outraged! When they went to bed she guarded the bedroom door to ensure he didn't come in. It wasn't until Mr Cooper had shut it that she could settle down at the end of the bed.

The next morning Mabel had a quick inspection and realised that Lucky had been weeing around the house, creating a most unpleasant odour. Then Lucky caught a mouse in the pantry, and Mrs Cooper made such a fuss saying how good he was. After breakfast they opened their Christmas presents and Lucky played with the wrapping paper and jumped in and out of the boxes. Everyone was saying how funny he was! Mabel sat quietly and was very unimpressed.

By the time Christmas lunch was being served Mabel needed a rest. She just wanted to nest in the sofa cushions, but it was not to be. Lucky pounced onto the table, prowled along the centre and scavenged a whole leg of turkey from the meat plate, right in front of everyone.

It was the final straw! Mabel couldn't tolerate any more outrageous behaviour. Using all her might she climbed up onto a chair and then stepped up onto the table, moving between the wine glasses and crockery,

and finally over the roast potatoes to confront Lucky.
But Lucky wasn't going to let go. He jumped over her,
landing on the wine glasses and spilling red wine over
the white tablecloth. Mabel gave chase, twisting back
along the table. Her paw landed in the bread pudding,
which was very hot and sticky. She had to get that leg
back – Lucky couldn't be allowed to get away with it!

When Mabel had reached the floor once more she wasn't sure where Lucky had gone, but she followed her nose. The smell of turkey led her to the drawing room, and there he was under the Christmas tree, chewing away on Mr and Mrs Cooper's lunch!

Mabel cornered him, and her jaws sank into the turkey meat, but Lucky tore it away and sprang up onto the first branch and then up to the next. The Christmas tree was shaking. Mabel decided this had to end. She leapt up too. It was the highest she'd jumped in a very long time, but the next branch was much closer. Lucky leapt higher still, and Mabel followed. The tree swayed, and baubles fell to the floor.

'Lucky, Mabel, stop!' Mrs Cooper shouted from the door, the guests appearing by her side.

Mabel reached the next branch and hissed at Lucky to stop, but on he soared. The tree lurched towards the window. Lucky was running out of branches to climb and had nowhere to go. Mabel was just inches away – if she stretched out one paw she'd have the turkey leg. With a *crunch* her teeth grasped it. She had saved the day!

But then Lucky, finding the tree had leaned over towards the sofa, dropped onto Mabel's cushion. The tree, now released of Lucky's weight, swung back, and back further still, and all of a sudden Mabel was flung out of the tree! She felt herself flying – it was a most strange feeling. Mabel looked around the room as she spread out her paws like wings. So this is what it was like to be a bird, she thought, before landing safely in Mr Cooper's arms. He caught her gently, holding her like a baby, and she dropped the turkey leg onto his chest.

Mabel had returned their lunch. All was good, and she was the proudest of cats. Mr Cooper held her for the rest of the day, even at supper time, and she had a bit of turkey from his fingers.

For Christmas Mabel got a little pet bed, which she used in the kitchen during the day. After Christmas life returned to normal, which was how she liked it – just her and Mr and Mrs Cooper.

Felicity, the Headmistress' Cat

Wasn't Mabel's Christmas adventure fun? But it's a shame she stays in the Manor House all the time, because she's missing out on meeting the other cats. I imagine she'd get on really well with Felicity, the headmistress' cat. You'll love her and Miss Pemberton, the headmistress, too! They are inseparable and adore each other. See what you think – we can go and call on them now.

Let's leave the Manor House from under the porch with its climbing roses. Give them a good sniff and then we'll turn left along the walled garden, cutting across the paddock to the half-timbered, thatched cottage. As we walk up the lane there's the pub on our right, and straight ahead is West Dean Primary School.

Miss Pemberton is the headmistress of the village school. She is a young lady who is patient, kind and pretty. The children love her and they love being in her class. She makes lessons fun by playing games, and she is always understanding if a child is struggling.

Miss Pemberton used to go to West Dean Primary School herself, and at the age of six decided that one day she'd like to be a teacher there. After college she went to university, and when she came back to the village the school board offered her the temporary position of 'Head Mistress' until they could find a suitable man to run the school. That's how it was back then, but do you think it was fair of the school board to assume a man would do a better job than Miss Pemberton? I'll tell you what Miss Pemberton did about it: she worked very hard in the school to make the children's schooldays as happy as her own. As a result the board made her position permanent, which means forever.

Miss Pemberton's cat is a ginger-brown cat with glassy green eyes. She is very pretty and playful and loves to be with people. Her name, Felicity, means 'happiness'. She has always been Miss Pemberton's cat, and they have never spent a day apart. Miss Pemberton even took her to lectures at university, hidden away in her shopping bag.

Felicity has a special dream that one day she will have a kitten that she can bring up and care for.

Miss Pemberton also has a special dream: she hopes of one day getting married and having a fairy-tale wedding. When she was young her aunty married the estate manager's son. They were allowed to have a party at West Dean Park, the big house on the other side of the wall. Nearly the whole village had come, and they had fancy food served on fine porcelain and eaten with silver cutlery. A band from London played music and they danced late into the midsummer's night. The guests explored the magical garden with its exotic plants and saw how the rich folk lived. It was like being a princess for a day, and Miss Pemberton never forgot that feeling.

One day Felicity and Miss Pemberton went to visit the Big House to talk to the estate's office about the upkeep of the school. There they met a very handsome cat named Eejay whose master, Edward James, was the owner of the Big House. The cat was friendly and played 'hunt and be hunted' with Felicity in the Great Marble Hall. Then he led her to his favourite spot by the French doors at the end of the long gallery, which overlooked the garden. Now Felicity often sees Eejay by the flint bridge where the river comes under the wall. Felicity loves their little strolls along the banks under the willows, but he never stays quite long enough.

Felicity and Miss Pemberton live opposite the school, just east of the railway line. They start each day together. Felicity has a little cot next to Miss Pemberton's bed, and when she has her cup of tea they sit in bed together. After breakfast they feed their tortoise, Charles. No one is quite sure how old Charles is, but he has been in the family for over 80 years and is thought to have come to England with the naturalist Charles Darwin, when he returned home from his voyage to the Galapagos Islands. Charles mostly sleeps as he is so old, but he will eat a bit of lettuce and tomato from Miss Pemberton's hand. When Felicity was a kitten she'd sit on his back and he'd give her piggyback rides, but she's too big for that now.

Miss Pemberton doesn't trust Felicity with the road, even though fewer than five cars or carriages may travel along the road each day, so she carries her in her arms to the school. Once they arrive, Felicity will sometimes follow Miss Pemberton about, but often she will just make her own way around, doing her own thing.

The children enjoy playing with the cat. They love to dress her up like a doll, with a little vest and cap. Felicity is quite happy if the children are gentle, but if they start to behave roughly she will wander off and return when they are calmer. They will put her in the doll's house, although she really is too big for that, and take it in turns to carry her. She will sit quietly as they push her around the playground in a pram. If she spots a child who is looking lonely, she will introduce herself by rubbing herself along their legs.

At the end of lessons and when they have said goodbye to the children, Felicity and Miss Pemberton will go upstairs to Miss Pemberton's office to deal with the letters and make phone calls. Afterwards they will go back home and have a relaxed supper together. Before bedtime Miss Pemberton takes a bath, which is one of the few things that Felicity will not do with her. Instead she sits quietly up on the shelf with the bath salts and bubble bath, or sometimes she will pop outside, especially if she hears her friend the Barn Cat meowing for her. Then it's lights out early so they are both fresh for the morning.

*

One day a Mr Woodrow was appointed to be teacher of the boys' class. Back then boys and girls only mixed in the infants' class, and after that they had separate classes with separate entrances and weren't allowed to mix in the playground. Miss Pemberton wanted to help Mr Woodrow as much as she could, as he was a new teacher and may have had some difficulties in his first few days. He was coming for a tour of the school, and when he knocked on the door Felicity ran to greet him as she did with all visitors. But Mr Woodrow did not stop to pet her or say hello. Perhaps he was nervous.

Miss Pemberton guided him around the school, making suggestions on how he could use the school facilities to make lessons fun and enriching for the children. Felicity followed them around, keeping her distance.

When Mr Woodrow walked into Miss Pemberton's office he was excited.

'You have your own office, Miss Pemberton!'

'Yes, it's a good place for preparing lessons, meeting parents and talking privately with the children, if necessary.'

'Well it is a very nice space. How convenient for you to have a private office. There is room for another desk, however, if you ever wanted to share.'

'Shall we wait and see, Mr Woodrow?'

She showed Mr Woodrow the assembly hall and explained that she liked to have all the children singing and dancing at least three times a week.

'Is that necessary, Miss Pemberton? Shouldn't we be making more time for the three Rs?' He meant arithmetic, reading and writing.

'I believe the children, Mr Woodrow, need some fun in the day. It helps them to concentrate.'

At the end of her tour Mr Woodrow said, 'Well, I must be getting back home; it's six miles for me to cycle home to Chichester. I gather you live next to the school, Miss Pemberton. You're very lucky – it's so convenient for you. Would you ever be looking for a lodger?'

Miss Pemberton was quite shocked at such a suggestion; in those days it would have been scandalous for a young man to be a lodger at the home of an unmarried woman. 'Shall we wait and see, Mr Woodrow?'

The next day Mr Woodrow gave his first lesson,

and he found things difficult. Miss Pemberton heard lots of shouting coming from his classroom but decided not to go in, thinking that he'd just need time to settle in. But then she saw the door open and Mr Woodrow was bringing Felicity out.

'Oh! Hello, Miss Pemberton. Do you think we ought to have cats in the classroom?'

'As you wish, Mr Woodrow. It's your classroom,' she said and, picking Felicity up, took the cat back to her own classroom. Felicity stayed quite close to her for the rest of the afternoon.

The next day the vicar, Reverend Harold Lyne, came to take his weekly assembly. As Mr Woodrow brought his children into the hall, he was shouting at Ben Dunk, 'No talking, boy – not unless you want to write out some lines for me!'

The vicar looked up and walked over. 'Hello, you must be the new teacher. I'm Father Harold, pleased to meet you.'

'Yes yes, nice to meet you too, but I'd like to get back to my class and my teaching as soon as we can.'

'Yes, of course,' the vicar replied.

After lessons, Father Harold came back to the school and asked to see Miss Pemberton in her office.

'Miss Pemberton, I am concerned. The boys didn't look happy in today's assembly. Do you think everything's as it should be with the new teacher? How much do you know about Mr Woodrow?'

Miss Pemberton thought about what she did know as she stroked Felicity on her lap.

The vicar continued, 'Do you think he'll fit in here?'

'Well, I'm not sure,' replied Miss Pemberton cautiously. 'We'll wait and see. Thank you for taking the time to come and talk with me, Father Harold.'

As Miss Pemberton walked home she thought about the vicar's words. She made supper and was just about to sit down to eat it when there was a knock at the door. Felicity, as usual, went to find out who it was and, as the door opened, they both saw Mr Woodrow. Felicity hissed and arched her back, her tail straight up in the air.

'Whatever is the matter, Felicity? You know Mr Woodrow!'

'You really do have quite a cat there, Miss Pemberton!' said Mr Woodrow.

'Yes, thank you. We are great friends. We go everywhere together, and she even has a bed next to mine.'

'Do you really have the cat in your bedroom?' asked Mr Woodrow incredulously. 'Don't you find that irritating?'

'Can I help you, Mr Woodrow? Was there something you were worried about?' asked Miss Pemberton.

'I came to see if you'd like to go to the cinema with me tomorrow night. There's a really funny movie about a couple that get married; they're both teachers in the same school.'

'Oh, how funny! Well I hope it's a big jolly wedding in a big country house.'

'Oh I don't know. If it were me, a quick drink at the local pub would be fine,' said Mr Woodrow.

'Well it's nice of you to ask me but I don't want to leave Felicity on her own,' Miss Pemberton said.

'She'll be okay for an evening. I'm sure she can catch a mouse or two if she's hungry.'

'Well not tomorrow, thank you, Mr Woodrow, but perhaps another time. We shall wait and see.'

The next day it was raining and windy. Many of the children came to school wet through, so Miss

Pemberton gave them towels to dry themselves with. There weren't enough towels for the children to have one each, but they shared and in the end everyone was happy. This was, however, the day that Miss Pemberton's 'waiting and seeing' regarding Mr Woodrow came to an end.

Miss Pemberton heard angry voices coming from the boys' class. Through the door she heard, 'Don't be ridiculous, boy!' She opened the door to find out what was going on, and that is when she saw it all. Mr Woodrow had opened a window, letting in the rain and wind, and was pushing Felicity out. 'Get out, you smelly cat,' he said.

'Mr Woodrow!' Miss Pemberton exclaimed. He stopped and turned to her. 'May I have a talk with you, please? Ben, can you please bring Felicity to me?'

Miss Pemberton stared at the disgraced teacher as he walked out of the classroom. She closed the door.

She stroked Felicity, who purred loudly as she held her in her arms. 'Mr Woodrow, I want you to look for employment elsewhere, is that understood?'

Mr Woodrow stared at Felicity, pushing his lips up towards his nose. 'It was the cat, wasn't it?'

'No, Mr Woodrow, it was you! Goodbye.'

Mr Cat and Mrs Cat of the Vicarage

Did you enjoy rubbing noses with Felicity? And wasn't Miss Pemberton brave? She took her time to decide about Mr Woodrow, but once she did she acted straight away.

Another kind person is the vicar, Father Harold. Let's say hello to him now, and while we are visiting him we can give Mr Cat and Mrs Cat a tickle. They live in the vicarage with the vicar and his wife, Florence. They are the most cordial, considerate and compassionate of cats, and you will find out why Mr Cat is a hero.

We'll leave the Headmistresses' house and head to the vicarage. Don't forget to close the gate behind you. Turning up the hill as though we're going to Midhurst or Cocking, the road cuts through the elm wood where the trees' leaves make a canopy; it's like walking through a leafy tunnel. Can you hear that cuckoo? At the top we'll turn right onto Church Lane, and there on our left is the vicarage: a well-proportioned building, white and smart.

Mr Cat and Mrs Cat love everything to be tidy, clean and in order. They wear purple elasticated collars with name badges. They are marmalade cats, with coarse-cut orange stripes that have golden highlights. There are no white boots, bibs or tail tips – they are pure marmalade.

Every morning chores must be done before they and their kittens can play. Mr Cat begins the day with a visit to the church to make sure everything is as it should be: locked doors and windows, closed gate and no feline or canine visitors in the churchyard.

To get to the church from the vicarage you or I would leave through a simple door cut into the tall flint wall and proceed down the narrow Church Lane to St Andrew's. Mr Cat takes a shorter route via the vicarage garden, with its ancient yew, and climbs over the fence at the end. It's so pleasant to see the glistening dew, the early snowdrops and crocuses, and to hear the melodic birdsong.

Before returning to Mrs Cat he will spring up the stairs of the belfry, to the top of the castellated tower with its four turrets, and admire the sunrise tipping over the downs into the valley of West Dean, like cream being poured from a jug. He will think of the day ahead and count his blessings. How lucky he is to enjoy his nine lives in such a lovely village.

Mrs Cat will be busy attending to the kittens. There is a feed and a clean to do, as well as the unending task of keeping them out of trouble. She is very thankful when Mr Cat returns to take over kitten control. She will then join the vicar and his wife for breakfast in the morning room which is next to the pantry. They will always put out extra food for Mrs Cat when she has a litter. The vicar will read his paper while Florence opens the morning post and advises him on any important matters.

'Harold, dear, Mr Morgan wants us to ask the parishioners to keep to the path as it's become rather muddy.'

'Will do, Flo. I'll mention it on Sunday at the 10 o'clock service.'

After a brief stroll in the vicarage gardens, Mrs Cat will return to the litter to help Mr Cat with the grooming. Often there will be a kitten that has wandered off to the library or larder and will need collecting. She will fetch them by picking them up gently from behind their necks with her mouth. Mr Cat will give the morning lesson. It might be silent walking, hunting or vocalising, which he displays with a mellow meow or gravelly growl. But he is careful not to frighten the kittens.

Mr Cat and Mrs Cat love to snuggle up and watch the kittens play. Mr Cat likes to clean Mrs Cat by licking behind her ears and checking her fur for any bugs or dirt she has picked up from the garden. And then Mr Cat will lick his paw and wipe it around his own head. He must spend over two hours a day with this preening!

Father Harold and his wife like to look in on the cats before lunch and will give them a stroke and a cuddle. They will name the kittens, even though they are to be given away. Usually they are the same names as the previous litter, since they are very fond of these names. Each name is a different brand of marmalade.

'Look, Flo, Chivers is trying to tackle Wilkin,' Father Harold said, pointing.

'And Duerrs is hiding behind Mr Cat.'

'Dundee and Coopers seem to still be hungry. Poor Mrs Cat.'

'Do you think Keiller has gone off again to the library?' Florence said.

'No, there's Keiller – it's Tiptree that's missing.'

Last year Mrs Cat's litter had been so large they added Fortnum and Mason to the list. Despite their love of these names, the vicar and Mrs Lyne will only eat marmalade made by Vera Smith, the church organist, as she chooses the best Seville oranges.

Mrs Cat likes to follow Florence around the vegetable patch as she collects the evening's supper and watch as she weeds, plants and tends to the growing food. The vicar is very busy looking after the neighbouring villages of Singleton, East Dean and Chilgrove, but when he is working at St Andrew's Mr Cat likes to go with him to the church. He walks beside him on the lane and doesn't cut through the yew hedge.

They will walk back together for the mid-morning pastoral care, where the vicar chats with parishioners about whatever is worrying them. Mr Cat likes to meet them as they are walking to the door, and if they are nervous or tense Mrs Cat will sit next to them or sometimes on their lap. Father Harold will meet them in the library, so it's easy for Mr Cat and Mrs Cat to help out.

The church is busy with its many weekly services: Holy Communion on a Sunday, Evensong and Morning Prayer. And then there are the weddings, christenings and funerals. Mrs Cat delights in watching the weddings; everyone is always so jolly and colourful. After the funerals, Mrs Cat will look out for people in the graveyard. If they are looking as if they are missing someone she will keep them company for a while.

In addition to all this there is the church calendar. It starts just before Christmas when the nativity scene is set out behind the font. Mr Cat will sometimes climb into the little model manger and sit on the hay. It is only the children who seem to notice him there. There is a mad rush to get the Christmas decorations down before Epiphany, as they believe it's unlucky if they are still up by then. This is the twelfth day of Christmas, when the Three Wise Men came to see baby Jesus.

Then at Easter there's the chocolate egg hunt. The vicarage gardens are open to let the children search for sweets hidden by Father Harold and Florence. Mr Cat enjoys escorting the children through the garden, showing them his favourite spots.

In August they will have the annual fête on the garden lawn. This is popular with the villagers, as well as the farm labourers, foresters, charcoal burners and people from the surrounding villages. There are tug-of-war games, competitions for best vegetable, cakes and pickles, coconut shies, a tombola and sometimes Morris dancers. Mr Cat and Mrs Cat find the occasion too raucous, especially if people bring their dogs. It is irritating for Mr Cat and Mrs Cat, as they can smell them for days afterwards.

In September there is the Harvest Festival, and this is the busiest time for the vicarage cats. Lots of food is delivered to the church in the weeks before. It will be blessed at the festival and then distributed to the poor. The trouble is that the food attracts the mice and rats, and Mr Cat and Mrs Cat are compelled to guard it day and night. It's such a relief when the festival is over.

The last big festival of the year is Advent, which celebrates the coming of Jesus. Candles are lit to symbolise the light of God. In 1934 Advent was on the 26th of November, a Monday. That was the day it all went wrong for St Andrew's and the parishioners of West Dean.

The day before, they'd had a ceremony to light the first candle of Advent. About 20 children were laying out the manger with its models of Jesus, Mary and Joseph, the Three Wise Men, and the farm animals. Vera Smith was practising the organ and had chosen Christmas hymns to make the children's visit festive and fun. Florence and Mrs Warner, the blacksmith's wife, were hanging up Christmas decorations. The church was looking wonderful.

Mr Cat stretched out on the hay, waiting for it to be moved into the manger, and then it happened: a small pillar of smoke curled up from the south transept, the place near the altar. The decorations were on fire!

Mr Cat leapt up and hurled himself into the manger, but the children just laughed. They didn't know he had seen the fire behind them tracing along the paper ribbons and up into the wooden roof beams. Mr Cat raced around the children trying to make them understand, but they were just laughing and pointing at him. The fire was spreading fast. Black smoke billowed from a stand of prayer books. Then he saw a red flame shoot up along the door frame. Mr Cat hurtled towards the organ. He needed to make them see! He jumped up Vera's back and landed straight on the keyboard. The thunderous blast made everyone look up.

'Fire!' Father Harold shouted. 'Everyone out!'

Vera tried to stamp on the Christmas decorations to put out the fire.

'It's too late, Vera! Call the fire brigade. I'll take the children.'

Vera sprinted to the Big House, West Dean Park, as they had a phone. The men of the village formed a line and passed buckets of water from the college to the church. The fire brigade was very swift, considering they had come from six miles away.

But there just wasn't enough water. The summer had been so dry the river was empty. All they could do was keep people away and watch as the fire surged and took possession of the church.

Father Harold led the children up the hill to the vicarage. In the garden he watched as his beautiful church turned to ash and rubble. Then they saw the roof collapse, and they heard a mighty clang as the bells crashed to the bottom of the tower. Mrs Cat tried to comfort Father Harold by sitting next to him; she had never seen him cry before.

Florence put her arm around him. 'Harold, my poor love.'

'Look at it, Flo, all gone. There wasn't time for me to save anything. All the paintings, the church treasures, that tapestry, gone!'

'Yes, but you saved the treasure.'

He looked at her.

'The precious children,' she said.

Father Harold realised she was right. 'Yes, Flo, we must thank God. It could have been so much worse.' He wiped a tear from his cheek. 'Thank the Lord Mr Cat went wild. You know, he must have seen the smoke first.'

It took a year and a half to rebuild the church; in the meantime the parishioners had to go to other villages for church services. Finally, when it was all done, there was a celebration, and Mr Cat could once more climb to the top of the belfry. Some wooden sculptures were lost but many of them were copied, and the church had brand new bells and an organ. The church calendar started again and Mr Cat and Mrs Cat returned to their duties.

Jaspurr the Pub Cat

Wasn't Mr Cat brave? It was such a disaster when the church burnt down, and only four days before St Andrew's day! If you go there now you would never know it ever happened, but there is a memorial stone on the wall to let people know that it did.

There's a story about one of Mr Cat and Mrs Cat's kittens, Max. We'll hear that later, but now it's time to drop in on Jaspurr, one of Spark's kittens. We've met him before when he was no bigger than your hand and had no name. Now he's nearly fully grown but is as playful as ever.

Ted Boxall, the Woodcutter, knew his cottage wasn't big enough for all of Spark's kittens. He had to find them homes in the village, and he thought it best if Jaspurr went first. Jaspurr was the one with the blue-grey coat and white bib and boots. He was too scared to play in the woods; he loved to scamper around the house instead, and he was the first to explore their home. He'd scratched a hole in the back of the sofa and made a den inside, and he'd shown his brothers and sisters how to climb up the curtain with just their claws. This little cat had outgrown the cottage.

Spark seemed to sense Jaspurr was leaving. She watched as the Woodcutter lowered him into the deep pocket of his wax jacket and she meowed a sad goodbye.

But Jaspurr was jubilant. It was dark and snug inside the pocket, with many smells: partridge, rabbit and something he hadn't smelled before on the Woodcutter's handkerchief. It was an odd motion riding on the bicycle. The chain squeaked like a mouse, and when he peeked out he saw the beautiful green hills. So Jaspurr left Whiteland Cottage, winding down Hasler's Lane, taking a sharp left at the main road and past Church Lane, and there opposite the school was the pub – his new home.

The pub was named The Selsey Arms. It was run by Ron Carter. He'd lived in the village all his life and had married Ada, the grocer's daughter, at St Andrew's a few years earlier. But Ron's dreams hadn't worked out and he found himself alone. Over the years the Woodcutter watched Ron's sadness deepen day by day, like the fungus on a damaged tree. The pub became dirty, and Ron grew quiet and somewhat grumpy. Often there wasn't any food to sell to the customers, as Ada had been the one to cook. Ted thought it would help if Ron had a kitten.

At the bar the Woodcutter waited for his pint to be poured. 'I've got a little surprise for you,' he said, opening his pocket.

As he passed Jaspurr to Ron he whispered in his ear, 'You were my favourite. You're wild like Mum.'

Ron couldn't put Jaspurr down, and the kitten purred so loudly it made everyone laugh. So Ron asked if he could keep him, and when Ted said yes Ron smiled and kept on smiling the whole day.

Jaspurr thought the pub was very smelly and gloomy inside. It was like being back in the Woodcutter's pocket, but it was cheery being around all the customers. Ron made a great fuss of Jaspurr and they spent much of the time together. Jaspurr had a favourite stool by the bar where he would preen his fur and watch Ron work. He liked the strokes and tickles the customers gave him. At night Ron put Jaspurr on his bed, at the end. Sometimes he'd stay but mostly he'd sneak away to explore.

Jaspurr sensed the presence of someone else at the pub; their scent was mostly in Ron's bedroom. It was the smell of summer, as if a hedgerow of buddleia had grown there. He knew the clothes in the wardrobe weren't all Ron's; some of them smelled like the honey the Woodcutter put on his toast.

Every Sunday Jaspurr and Ron strolled down to a walled garden with standing stones, all in lines. Each stone had writing on it. Ron always went to the same one and would sit there and talk. Then he'd lay flowers and say goodbye, stroking the top of the stone

as he left.

There were lots of buildings in the village and lots of places to go. As Jaspurr explored further down the lane, past the shop, he found a green with a flint bridge over a river. He could tell by the smell that many cats had been there, and it wasn't long before he got to play with Felicity, Eejay and the Barn Cat.

Jaspurr liked to discover and try new things, but it didn't always go to plan. The first time he walked out past the flint bridge, next to Harcourt House, he was startled by a herd of cows behind him.

They'd come out from their afternoon milking. The first few cows charged at him and he had to sprint across the river, getting soaked through. Then there was the time when he'd jumped up onto the bar and landed on a tray of glasses. The tray launched across and off the bar, and he'd done a backflip. He'd landed on his paws, of course, but the glasses smashed on the floor. Ron wasn't angry, he was only worried for Jaspurr.

Despite being the son of the Woodcutter's cat, Jaspurr was not a natural hunter. He was content with a tin of Gaines cat food and, in fact, had come to love it.

Ron would say, 'What will we do if we run out of Gaines? That would be a CAT-astrophe, wouldn't it, Jaspurr?' Then he'd giggle.

After a couple of months Ron spotted mouse droppings in the cellar. 'Right, Jaspurr, it's time to do your job!' So he took him down into the dingy room. However, when Jaspurr saw the mouse he scarpered.

Fortunately for Ron, Jaspurr and the Barn Cat had become great friends. When they'd first met, Jaspurr started play fighting and the Barn Cat, despite his great age, played along too. The Barn Cat realised that Jaspurr needed to learn about hunting, and one day turned up with a mouse hanging by its tail from his mouth. Jaspurr was curious and watched as the Barn Cat had his meal. Then the next day the Barn Cat turned up with a live mouse and dropped it in front of Jaspurr. The Barn Cat acted out a hunting scene, pricking up his ears, turning to a statue and then snatching the mouse.

*

One day a large lady came bustling into the pub, out of breath and rosy with the Easter sun.

'Hello, Ron, my love. Do you remember me?'

'Ruby! Ruby, the Land Girl! How are things up in London?' Ruby had laboured at Manor Farm during the war but had loathed the work and gone back home.

'Well, things haven't worked out too well. I thought I'd try my luck back here again. Not farming, you'll be pleased to hear,' she giggled. 'I need some work for a while and a place to stay… just till I get set up in Chichester.'

'Well, I do need someone to get the place up together; it's fallen a bit behind. But there's no chaperone, mind!'

'I ain't no lady,' she said, laughing as she slapped the bar. 'And I'm old enough to look after myself.'

'Well…'

'I'll be no trouble and I'll get this place sparkling. Just give us a chance!'

'Well, there is the kitchen put-you-up. I can have that and you can have my bed.'

'That's settled then, but I ain't pushing you out of your bedroom. I'll take the put-you-up.'

Within minutes Ruby was filling a bucket to spring clean the filthy pub.

Then she saw Jaspurr and exclaimed 'Ooh, who's this gorgeous fella?' And she made a fuss of him.

Ruby was different from Ron. Where he would wait for the right thing to say, Ruby liked to speak straight away, and usually it was something that made people laugh. And she did like to laugh herself! When she started, everyone around her laughed too. Ruby greeted the customers with a 'Hello, love' or a 'Lovely morning, isn't it?' and as they left she would thank them and say 'Have a lovely day' or 'Wrap up tight – it's cold tonight.'

She would play the piano, which she called Joanna, and get the whole pub singing with her while Jaspurr sat on top.

Ruby also pumped the beer up from the cellar. Ron had offered to do it but Ruby said, 'I've got arms, haven't I? Thank you anyway, my lovely. You go and rest up.'

One day the Woodcutter came for his weekly visit to see Jaspurr and for his drop of ale.

'Morning, Ron. I'll have a pint, please.'

'Ah, I'm sorry, Ted, the beer's all gone!'

Ted was speechless.

'Ha ha, gotcha,' Ron said, chuckling.

'Well it's good to see you so chipper again. So tell me, who's the cause of that, Jaspurr or Ruby?' Ron went bright red, and that's when he realised he had changed.

*

Just before Easter the Barn Cat and Jaspurr had their first proper hunting trip. Jaspurr wasn't quite fully grown but his claws were sharp. They'd had a

71

few night trips over the wall in the gardens of the Big House, watching the dovecote with its yummy birds and waiting for the squeak of a mouse underneath the thatched grain store. The Barn Cat was an experienced hunter and showed Jaspurr how to crouch low, move on his belly and make no sound.

One cold night they had set off as the pub was closing. When everyone else was finishing their day, the Barn Cat and Jaspurr were starting theirs. The moon shone brightly as they went past the flint bridge and back once more over the wall. When they landed they heard the startled cry of a pheasant, which made a rook and a jackdaw fly off.

Jaspurr heard the snap of a twig. What was that? He looked up and there was Mr Fielder, the head gamekeeper with his gun. Jaspurr hurtled away. He heard the gun blast behind him and the shot peppered the bush in front of him. He darted to the right before hearing a deafening second bang. He kept on running, deeper into the woods, down unknown paths. Finally, when he was out of breath, he stopped and stood quietly, waiting to recover.

Then there came the smell of something new, pungent and alien. It was like a cat but also like a dog. Jaspurr was puzzled. What could it be? Could he eat it? In front of him a large figure emerged, breathing heavily and looking at him. Jaspurr understood: he wasn't the one hunting, he was being hunted!

It was a fox, its mouth open and snarling, baring as many teeth as the Woodcutter's saw. The moonlight glinted in the fox's black eyes. It pounced. Jaspurr sprang into the air. The fox's teeth grabbed his ear and he felt the fox's leg kick his belly. Jaspurr landed on the ground and set off in one movement, bolting through the undergrowth to an old tree. He clawed his way up with the fox right behind him. Feeling a sharp tug on his tail, Jaspurr leapt up further, tearing his tail from the fox's mouth. The fox could not grip the tree and flopped to the ground.

Jaspurr picked his way to the first branch he could sit on and froze so he could listen, but all he could hear was his own heart thumping. He felt his ear stinging and knew it was bleeding. He wanted to go home but he knew the fox was still there. He heard it breathing at the base of the tree, but when he looked into the darkness, even with his night vision, he couldn't see anything. Jaspurr felt his bruised belly – was that cut too? He gave it a lick. It seemed okay, but Jaspurr was still worried. How long would he have to wait? Would the fox find a way up to him? Had the Barn Cat escaped the gamekeeper's gun?

Suddenly, from out of the blackness he heard a cat's horrible hiss and a fox's grating growl, followed by a thud, the swipe of a claw and one set of paws fleeing away. Jaspurr waited. Who was left? Then he heard the most beautiful sound: 'Meow.'

In seconds he was down the tree, brushing his whiskers against the Barn Cat's, which in cat means 'thank you'.

Jaspurr pushed through his pet door and limped to the glowing embers of the fire. He was tired and shaken and wanted to sleep.

'Ooh, Jaspurr! What's happened to you? Ron, come and see.' Ruby picked him up, and although it hurt his bruised belly Jaspurr purred.

Ron came down the stairs, two steps at a time, and put his arm around them both. 'Oh dear, he has been in the wars!'

Ruby passed Jaspurr to Ron. 'I'll get a cloth from the kitchen and clean up his ear before it gets infected. I might have to use TCP,' she said as she went to the kitchen.

'Well done, love,' Ron called out, and then whispered in Jaspurr's ear. 'I got some great news. You've got a new mum. Ruby and I are gonna be married. She says she'd like kids, too. She's bringing you some TCP, which will sting, I'm afraid. But you know, the best medicine is laughter – love and laughter. So I think we're going to be alright.' And with that he tickled Jaspurr under his chin. Of course Jaspurr didn't understand what Ron had said, but he liked the fuss all the same.

Jaspurr licked his wounds that night, which hurt quite a bit and didn't taste very nice with the TCP, but he remembered his adventure with glee and realised how good a friend the Barn Cat was. One day he hoped to be as brave as him, and he wondered what the next lesson in hunting would entail. As his mind curled up into dreamland he thought of the Woodcutter and Mum and imagined they'd be quite proud of him now that he was a hunter.

Max the Shop Cat

Jaspurr and the Barn Cat had quite an adventure, didn't they? It's so lucky for Jaspurr that they are such good friends. Our next tale is another story about their friendship. This one is about the time they had a snack at the village shop that wasn't theirs to eat. Naughty cats! In this story we'll meet Max, the Shop Cat, who was troubled by his missing tail. Let's see how his heart grows lighter by the end of this feline tale.

Max was not like his mum or dad, the pure marmalades of the vicarage. When he was born everyone was a little baffled: he had no tail and was not marmalade. His fur had black bits, white bits, a little brown here and patches of orange there, with no hint of a pattern. Mr Cat and Mrs Cat were quite puzzled.

Their distress, however, was forgotten when Mrs Bell, the sub-postmistress, delivered an important telegram. She parked her bicycle and knocked on the door. The vicar answered and opened the note straight away. It read:

CHURCH REBUILD APPROVED.

The vicar turned to look for his wife and tell her the great news, and that was when Mrs Bell spotted Max behind him, playing with his brothers and sisters.

'Ooh, a Manx moggie. Isn't he lovely!'

The vicar smiled. 'Would you like him, Mrs Bell?'

'Can I? He's gorgeous!' Mrs Bell left her bicycle at the vicarage and carried Max home. She walked down the narrow way, with its high flint walls, towards St Andrew's and then around the bend into sleepy Church Lane by the River Lavant. She stopped at West Dean General Stores, Max's new home.

Mrs Bell had realised straight away, as soon as she saw him, that Max was special. She knew his ancestors came from the Isle of Man, an island nestled between England, Wales, Scotland and Ireland. It is the home of a special kind of cat: the Manx. These cats don't have a tail but they do have a very particular nature. You can say, without joking, that they make great guard dogs, and that is exactly what Mrs Bell wanted. Max was now the Shop Cat, and his job was to help Mr and Mrs Bell – Lilian and Frank – run the busy shop.

At the heart of every village is its shop, and West Dean is no exception. It is a place where people catch up on local news, like who is getting married or having children, who is new to the village and who's bought whose horse. And Lilian and Frank do love to chat. They are very interested in everything that everyone has to say.

More importantly, the shop is the place where you

can buy everything you need. You could instead travel to Chichester but that is seven miles away, an hour by horse and carriage. So you can see the shop provides a great service to the villagers.

Lilian and Frank have two children: Elsie, who is six, and Robert, who is five. They love to play with their new kitten, and Max loves to play with them. He joins in with Robert's favourite game of hide and seek and tries the trick of walking on two legs for Elsie's circus. He can nearly do it! When they go to bed they take it in turns to have him under the covers with them. Max waits until they fall asleep before he sneaks away.

Max spends his days supervising the deliveries and patrolling the shop, repeating his tour every couple of hours. He checks that the doors are closed and that the garden is free of cats, and he makes sure that all dogs are on a lead. He knows that everything has a place and must be in its place. Max walks right around the shop, thinking of the places where different creatures may sneak in. A constant worry is the mice who love the shop because it's full of lovely things to eat.

Max is an expert on the shop's routine sounds: the stomp of Ben Dunk's father passing by before sunrise when he goes to fetch the cows for milking, the roar of the delivery lorry on a Thursday, the ring of the cash register, the purr of the machine slicing bacon and the rumble of coal tumbling into the cellar. He's also an expert on the smells in the shop: the aroma of fresh bread each morning and the mouth-watering scent of Elphick's sausages that the butcher brings on a Monday.

The one thing about Max that he doesn't want you to know is that he has no tail. It's his little secret. Of course, it's not a very good secret because everyone can tell he has no tail. It wasn't until he was almost a year old that Max realised he wasn't like the other cats. Where had his tail gone? Maybe a door had closed on it, or maybe he lost it in a fight. He struggles to remember! Maybe his dad was a rabbit?

It is such a worry for him. From the kids' room Max has a perfect view of the flint bridge by the green, and he can see the other cats playing. They are having so much fun, but he'll never go there. Would they talk to a cat with no tail? Even though Max believes the other cats will never accept him, and that makes him sad, he copes very well with his little secret. Life continues, with or without a tail.

Elsie and Robert play with Max when they come back from school and will keep him busy playing fetch or have him sit with them while they listen to their favourite radio show, *Singing Together*.

Sometimes Ben Dunk comes into the shop, usually on an errand for his mum, holding the list she has written. He likes to play with Max, and he speaks cat. This involves slowly blinking, which cats see as a sign of friendship. He makes a little exchange of scent by stroking Max's head and finally presents his nose for Max to rub with his. Ben learnt to speak cat while playing with his own cat, Aloysius, who is almost as big as Ben's other pet, a Jack Russell named Sally. Other customers want to stroke Max too, but Max will only let a few do that.

There are many children that come to the shop for their sweets, before or after school. They take paper bags and select each sweet carefully from the little boxes, and then Mr Bell works out how much money they cost. Max ensures there is no pre-sales tasting.

Mr Bell and Max work closely together. If Mr Bell shouts 'MAX, KEYS!' then Max will fetch the keys from the desk. If he shouts 'MAX, DOOR!' Max will push the door closed. So many customers leave the door open! Also, Mr Bell has a special whistle. He can make the sound of an owl, which goes 'twit twoo'. Whenever he makes this call, Max will come running, but Mr Bell once got into trouble when a customer thought he was whistling at her. Mr Bell will allow dogs to enter the shop, but Max won't – not one paw may pass through the door. The owners have to leave their dogs outside, tied to the porch. Mr Bell leaves a bowl of water out for them, which Max enjoys too.

Max loves water, which is unusual for a cat. One time he swam in the children's bath and made them laugh when he jumped out and shook the water off his fur, splashing them and the walls. Mrs Bell was not pleased that everything got so wet, so from then on Max wasn't allowed in at bath time. In the summer, though, when it's hot and sticky, he'll have a dip in the river and have some fun chasing the ducks.

One of Max's morning duties is to walk Robert and Elsie to school. He walks just ahead of them, leading the way. It's only a short walk up the lane, then he watches them wave goodbye before they go inside. On his return he often sees one or two cats playing by the green. It would be lovely to join them, but what would they think of a cat like him? Besides, he has his work to do.

*

One moonlit Friday night the Barn Cat and Jaspurr decided to see what was on offer at the shop. On Fridays the shop sold fish, and the lovely smell had enveloped the shop. The pair of cats had thought of nothing else all day and hoped that when the shop closed there would still be some left.

Skulking at the end of the path they saw Max come out of his pet door and take a tentative sniff. They were downwind of Max, so he went around the corner on his usual patrol.

The Barn Cat sprinted to the pet door and, once inside, followed his nose to the cold cabinet. Jaspurr stayed outside keeping a lookout. The Barn Cat saw two long fish in the cabinet, his mouth drooling at the thought of munching them, but he couldn't get in! There was a glass door but it wouldn't open with the push of a paw. Maybe there was a way in from the top. He jumped up but landed on a small saucer. Onto the ground it fell, and the sound of it smashing roused Max into action. He came running back and was going to jump through his pet door when he saw Jaspurr.

'Hiss!' went Max.

'Grrrooowwwouuu,' went Jaspurr.

Max went to jump on Jaspurr but Jaspurr sprang onto a water butt and then up a wooden drainpipe. Within seconds he was on the roof, dashing up to the top. He stood on the ridge and waited. Max appeared and charged towards him.

'Hiss!' went Jaspurr.

'Grrrooowwwouuu,' went Max.

Jaspurr went down the other side of the roof and then jumped onto the shed and off into the flowerbed. He waited there, but Max didn't follow.

Seeing Jaspurr leave, Max ran back to the shop. Who was inside?

The Barn Cat, knowing he'd probably been heard, decided to take anything he could find. He followed his nose: sausages! Ooh, and chicken too. But then, what was that over there? Pork pie!

Having heard Max hiss outside, he had to decide on one treat straight away. He sank his teeth into the sausage and lifted it out of the cabinet. Something was wrong – it was too heavy! It wasn't just one sausage, it was a long chain of them. The Barn Cat jumped to the ground, and as he ran the chain dragged on the floor between his legs.

He jumped through the pet door, but – oh no! – he was caught. The sausages were trapped in the flap. Then he heard Max growling on the roof. He didn't have long – Max was scrambling down.

'Oi, you!' It was Mr Bell tapping at the window. 'Lilian, the Barn Cat's got our sausages!'

Max landed on the ground and the Barn Cat gave one last tug. Two sausages broke off and he sprinted away.

Max didn't give chase; he stood guarding the other sausages, which were lying on the floor.

The door opened and Mr Bell appeared in his pyjamas. 'Well done, Max, you stopped them!' He picked up Max and gave him a kiss. 'Well I never! I can't believe that Barn Cat was so cheeky. Well protected, Max!'

When it had gone quiet, the Barn Cat found Jaspurr

by the flint bridge and they scoffed their winnings.

In the morning Max was celebrating his victory. Mrs Bell had poured him some cream and put out a bit of fish for him to nibble. She only did that on special occasions.

Max was very pleased with himself and took some time off to stroll around the shop. It was then that he found himself staring at a magazine cover as intently as he would a bird or mouse. It was a picture of a family of cats, and as he peered more closely he realised none of them had tails. Max stared at the picture, trying to make sense of it. Could this be true? They couldn't all have lost their tails – they must have been born like him without a tail! He realised then that he wasn't alone and that he was normal. He came from the same family of cats as the ones in the magazine.

So Max was different from most cats but not abnormal, just special. He put a paw up onto the picture to make sure it was real.

Max tore out of the pet door and galloped down to the green. As he had hoped, Jaspurr was there play fighting with the Barn Cat. And so, fulfilling his dreams, Max joined in too. He laid on his back, keeping his claws hidden, and Jaspurr pretended to pounce on him like a leaping leopard, although he was really very gentle. Then a few minutes later a lovely cat called Felicity arrived and joined their game.

It was so much fun, and now Max goes there every day. Once or twice a week Eejay comes too, making it quite a party.

Although they are all friends now, the shop still needs to be protected and Max cannot let the others inside – not even to see what is on offer.

José the Old Barn Cat

It was lovely that Max made friends with the other cats. And Jaspurr and the Barn Cat, what a pair! I think they may be my favourites. What about you? Wait – don't decide just yet! You haven't met Eejay yet, not properly. Before you do, let me tell you more about the Barn Cat. We've come across him quite a bit by now, but this story shows how little we sometimes know about our cats.

You say goodbye to your cat as you leave for school and when you get back they look just the same. Maybe they're even still sitting in the same place, but they may have had a busy, adventurous day. They can't tell you, of course, so you'll never know what they got up to, however adventurous. No one in West Dean knows that the Barn Cat was born in another country, not even Ben Dunk.

José, the old Barn Cat, lives on Manor Farm, where we met Mabel. Let's leave the shop and head down to the river and follow the direction of the water. It's not far. You can smell the barn before you see it, there, on your right before the slurry pit. In the barn you'll find the hay, the cows, the horses and the milk parlour. It's a busy place, with the cows going to and from the field to be milked twice a day. There's only one person in the village that calls the old Barn Cat by his real name and that's Ben Dunk, the son of the head cowman of Home Farm. The villagers know that the Barn Cat is black and white, quite old and catches lots of mice, but there's so much more they don't know!

Despite his Spanish name the Barn Cat was actually born in France, in a warehouse on the banks of the River Seine, where boats docked and unloaded their goods for the merchants of Paris. His mother was an expert mouse-hunter, which was useful for the warehouse owners as she protected the grain that was stored there. José and his siblings would play nearby in the Jardin des Tuileries.

The Jardin des Tuileries is a large park with trees the cats could climb and benches where people sat and picnicked. Sometimes the picnickers would feed the cats pieces of cheese and sausage, but there were also dangers lurking in the park. The worst fright they had occurred one afternoon when they were still kittens: two ferocious dogs ran towards them. Out sprang Mum; she knew that if you ran from a dog they'd run after you, so she stood her ground, arching her back, hissing and showing her claws. Once they saw how determined she was the dogs turned and walked away.

The kittens grew into cats but never lost their adventurous spirit. One day the Barn Cat smelled a wonderful whiff of cheese being carried on the back of a cart. It was being taken to the market, up the hill to the village of Montmartre. He followed his nose and found the lovely village overlooking Paris.

There were many artists, jugglers, dancers and singers performing in the street, and a crowd of people had gathered to watch the performers and buy things from the market stalls. The Barn Cat stayed by these stalls, living on the traders' scraps, until one day a man stopped to say hello, tickling him under his chin. Every day when the man went to the bakery he'd make a fuss of him, giving him some of his sandwich and stroking him. When the winter came he let him move into his apartment.

The man was called Pablo Picasso, and he was an artist. He sold his pictures so he could buy food and pay the rent. All he seemed to do was paint. He never went out to the theatre or movies, but people were always coming to see him. The Barn Cat had a bed under the easel and grew to enjoy the smell of linseed oil, varnish and turpentine. Pablo would put the Barn Cat on the laps of his models to keep them still while he painted them.

Pablo hosted big parties, and all the guests would make a fuss of the Barn Cat. One man, Monsieur Matisse, asked Pablo if he could take the cat home, but Pablo was quick to say no! When it got too loud the cat would find a quiet spot on the balcony, among the geraniums in terracotta pots, and he would look down on the vineyard and chestnut trees.

At one of these parties a lady had brought a large poodle with a strange haircut. It looked like someone had put a wig on it and put its legs through the centre of lots of bread rolls. The dog looked very nervous and, upon meeting the Barn Cat, decided to attack. First, he yapped and hurtled round in a circle between everyone's legs. Then he crouched down in front of the Barn Cat and, just as he was about to pounce, the cat swiped with his claw and scratched the poodle's nose. The dog ran off yelping and whining.

Pablo knelt and stroked the Barn Cat. The cat's fearlessness reminded him of the famous Spanish bullfighter José Gómez Ortega. 'Ah, my little man,' he said. 'It looks as though you have found your name. We will call you José.' From then on, whenever he painted pictures of José he made him look like a tiger, with stripes and with sharp claws and teeth.

At mealtimes Pablo would feed José fish from his fingers and let him lick his plate after supper. When he danced, he'd hold José like a baby and sing to him,

'*Todo lo que puedas imaginar es real*,' which is Spanish for 'Everything you can imagine is real.' Of course, José didn't understand the words, but he enjoyed it all the same. Pablo would kiss José on the nose each night, and that made José feel like a king. Life could not be better.

Sadly, it could not last forever. One day Pablo decided to move back to Spain. He took José to the river in a basket and gave him to his friends, Henri and Marie, who lived on a barge.

Their boat took goods along the French canals and rivers, delivering coal to the cities in the winter and collecting grain and fresh vegetables from the countryside in the summer.

José slept in a cubbyhole above Henri and Marie's bed, just on the other side of the stove so it was always warm and snug. He liked to sit with Henri as he fished from the side of the barge while Marie steered the barge along the waterway. He'd watch the fish dance on the end of the line, sparkling in the sunshine. It was a little dangerous being so close to the water, but in all their years together José never had to swim. He can, of course – he'd just rather not.

Marie painted the boat green, red and gold in a flower pattern. She covered pots and pans too, which she and Henri were able to sell in the markets. At night they would tie up against the quay and José could explore. Sometimes other boat owners would come on board to eat and play games. Henri played the accordion and Marie would sing. Every day they went to a different town, and as the years went by the Barn Cat saw the whole of France.

One summer's day José had spread himself out on top of the barge's roof to keep cool, and he awoke to the delicious aroma of fish. He jumped up and looked around to find that they were back in the port of Le Havre. It was the fishing boats that he smelled. Cod, mullet, prawn, plaice and scallops were being taken off the boat to the quayside. José had to follow his nose. He jumped aboard one of the larger boats and soon found a pile of fish heads. After filling his belly he snuggled into the middle of a coiled rope and, as he soaked up the coastal sun, fell asleep.

Hours later he lifted his head to see where he was.

The boat was at sea!

'*Regarde – un chat!*' shouted one of the fishermen.

Luckily, the fishermen could see the funny side of having a cat aboard, but they assumed he was a wild cat and not one with a family, so they didn't take him back to the port. Henri and Marie waited for nearly a week for their cat to return, but they knew deep in their hearts that José had started a new adventure and wouldn't be coming back to them.

The fishermen made a home for him in the galley. It was warm there and he was fed well every day. Life on board was just like the barge but with waves. When it was windy the boat was thrown about, so José looked for a special place to keep safe and found the captain's hammock. In the winter the captain would share the hammock with him and they'd keep each other warm. The crew kept José safe, not letting him go up on deck if the waves were too big, since there was no life jacket that would fit José. Back in port the captain would take him home to stay with his wife, Jacqueline. She loved José, and every time the captain returned to sea she would want José to stay, but the captain and the crew couldn't be without their cat.

It was like that for many years until a storm changed everything. They were near the coast of Southend-on-Sea and the wind was so strong it had blown the ship's flag away. Their engine had stopped working, and the crew knew they were in big trouble as the boat drifted towards the rocky coast. They had to be towed to London for repair.

José wasn't allowed out of the cabin. All he could do was look out of the porthole at the busy dockyard. But when the captain went out of the cabin he left the door ajar, and José leapt ashore. London was beautiful. The people spoke and dressed very differently to those he'd seen in France, but the buildings were tall like the ones in Paris. José followed his nose and eventually he came across a huge building guarded by a tall fence and men wearing strange hats that looked like bears. José went through the fence and explored the gardens. He came across two girls who took a fancy to him straight away, stroking and petting him.

'Lizzie, he's mine! I saw him first.'

'No, Maggie. *I* did, actually, and he seems to prefer me.'

José had run straight into Princess Elizabeth and her sister, Princess Margaret. But he couldn't wait to find out who would win as he was being chased by a pack of corgis. This wasn't a problem, as he could run rings around them, but the chase attracted the attention of the guards and he was shown out onto the busy road.

It had been quite some time since José had eaten and, recognising the sound of a railway station, he went looking for food. It was Victoria Station, which was very busy. He had to be careful the rushing travellers didn't walk on top of him as it was difficult to hear them coming over the roar of the steam trains. Then he saw lunch: a little rat scampering along the side of the waiting room. José gave chase through the ticket stall and onto the platform, then alongside a long line of carriages. The rat was quick and jumped up onto a train. José leapt onto the train too, but the rat had disappeared. Hungry and exhausted, José found a spot under a seat and soon fell asleep.

When he awoke it was morning. The train was on the move and he had been so tired that the noise and movement of the train leaving the station hadn't woken him up. José looked out of a window, and there was the countryside: tall trees, long hedges, little villages and fields of green. When he saw a river he thought of how thirsty he was, and so he jumped out of the window and ran towards the water.

And that is the story of how the Barn Cat found his way to West Dean. As soon as he had quenched his thirst in the cool water he found the barn, which reminded him of his first home – the warehouse in Paris. The barn gave José the freedom he loved, with no doors and no oceans with waves. He'd found his piece of paradise. Soon afterwards he met Ben Dunk, who would always feed him tasty morsels from his pocket, so he decided to stay.

One day the following summer, when he was hunting in the Big House's gardens, he heard someone calling his name. It was the first time he'd heard it in 12 years. It was Pablo, who was walking by with Eejay's master. He was much older and heavier than he'd been when José last saw him in Paris, and his hair was grey, but José knew it was him. Pablo made a big fuss of José, stroking and hugging him, and then kissing him on the nose. José felt like a king again. Pablo gave him one last hug and walked away. This was when Ben saw the exchange and heard Pablo call the Barn Cat 'José'.

To Pablo, the Barn Cat was only a cat that looked like the cat he'd had in Paris. He would never have believed that José could have travelled the hundreds of miles from France to West Dean. But if José could have spoken he would have told Pablo his story.

Often when José sleeps his paws and tail twitch. This is him dreaming, remembering a lifetime of adventures. It could be that his days of following his nose are over... or maybe they're not.

Eejay and the Cat Competition

Could you have guessed the Barn Cat was born in France? What an adventurer! As a cat that loves to travel, do you think he'll stay in West Dean? He is quite elderly now. Either way, don't worry – you haven't heard the last of him.

We're nearly at the end of the book now, and you

still haven't spent any time with Eejay, who lives in the Big House!

If we leave the barn on Manor Farm and walk along the river, past Mr Bell's shop and the flint bridge, we'll find ourselves walking along a tall flint wall. It begins on the main road into West Dean and runs all the way through until it's almost at the top of the Trundle. It is part of the Monarch's Way, which was the escape route taken by King Charles II in 1651 after he was defeated in the Battle of Worcester. But that's another story. Near the church is a plain door cut into the wall. Because it is so plain it's easy to ignore, but if you know what's on the other side you'll want to slink through.

Walking through the door is like visiting another kingdom: a place where visiting kings are entertained at big parties, a place where Rolls-Royces purr, poets dream and artists paint. The huge flint house stands before you. It has the presence of a castle and the lure of a palace. This is Eejay's magical home, West Dean Park.

Eejay likes to talk a lot, and at the Big House there are lots of people to talk with. He asks for what he wants and tells people what he thinks and what they should be doing. No one completely understands what he's saying though, so much is lost in translation.

He has five types of meow:

For 'Hello', it's 'Me-OW'.

For 'I'm hungry', it's 'Meeeow'.

For 'Can you take my collar off?' it's 'Meoooow'.

For 'Please open the door', it's just 'Meow'.

For 'Why is that silly dog in here?' it's 'Meowwww'.

See! You can hear the difference, can't you? And don't forget the purring, of which there are three varieties:

For 'You're warm', it's 'Purr'.

For, 'Don't stop, that feels good', it's 'Purr, rrr, rrr'.

For, 'Shall we just stay like this, until I fall asleep?' it's 'Purr mmm'.

And then, of course, there are Eejay's other voices: the yowling, chirping, snarling and growling. Each one is used to get different messages across.

Eejay wears a collar with a silver medallion. On one side is his name and on the other is written, 'Care of West Dean Park'. But there really is no need, for everyone knows Eejay. He's the only Siamese in the village. His looks are famous – the way his blue eyes inspect you, talk to you and hold you under their spell.

Eejay has certain standards he likes to maintain. He only drinks from a saucer, and the water must be fresh. He likes to have the full attention of any person he is sitting with, and he can't abide the bark of a dog – it's so, well, irksome.

Eejay, like most Siameses, is a thinking cat, and he has his own philosophy. You may question whether a cat can have a such a thing, but when you hear Eejay's you'll know that they can, and you'll understand cats a lot better too.

Eejay's philosophy: cats have independent thought. They'll listen to your wishes but make up their own minds as to what they will do. They are nocturnal; sunshine is for sleeping in. Cats are not pack animals. They are solitary hunters and they don't understand the idea of a team. Friendship with anyone may be brief! If it's good: stay. If it's bad: leave. They also believe that one must laugh at the working dog – they are very foolish to work so hard and be so obedient.

For Eejay the Big House doesn't feel like a home. The rooms are designed to be impressive, with their grand fireplaces, tall ceilings, huge tapestries and fancy columns. There are too many guests who try to make their introduction by petting him unannounced. And the Great Marble Hall, with its stuffed animal heads on the wall! That is strange to see – are they dead or alive?

Eejay prefers to be in the servants' quarters; they have a small fire and he can sit on Ben Dunk's lap. Ben is the only child who helps out at the Big House; he sometimes stays over in the servants' quarters. He plays with Eejay and feeds him.

West Dean Park is owned by a very rich and thoughtful man, Edward James. He lives there from time to time, but mostly he lives somewhere between the world of what he sees and hears and his own imagination.

Edward stays at West Dean less and less often, as he prefers Monkton House nearby. That's where he and Eejay used to live together, along with a beautiful lady called Tilly who brought Eejay to England from Austria. Eejay would sit on Edward's lap each night while Edward read him poetry and talked about the book he was writing.

The house was cosy but a little odd; it had a sofa in the shape of a pair of lips and an aquarium in the bathroom. Eejay loved to look at the fish but in the end was very pleased to move out, as an Irish wolfhound had moved in and he was terrifying. Once the dog put his front paws on Edward's shoulders and stood on his back legs, and that made him taller than Edward! Also, it was more fun at the Big House, as it had lots of people who would stop and say hello.

Eejay is Edward's cat, but Eejay feels like he really belongs to Ben Dunk. One time in the garden Edward had called to Eejay but Eejay went to Ben instead. Ben was embarrassed but Edward said, 'Don't worry, I'm being punished for being away so much. Eejay needs someone he can see every day, and so I thank you for that,' and he gave Ben a 10-shilling note, which was a lot of money!

'Wow, thank you kindly,' Ben said. 'There's enough here to help all the cats. You should see some of them in the winter – they really suffer!'

'Well, all the farms need the cats, Ben. So if you need anything else just tell Mr Morgan. Say I sent you.'

'Thank you, Mr James! My teacher said you were a true gentleman.'

'Well, that is good to hear, Ben. You know, I may appear generous but I have so much to give. They say it is easier for a camel to pass through the eye of a needle than it is for a rich man to enter the Kingdom of Heaven.'

*

In the summer, Miss Bond, a relative of Edward's, came to stay in the Big House. She was from Florida, in the United States of America, and she was very passionate and energetic and loved almost everything about England. She had brought her horse across the ocean to race at Goodwood, which is just over the hill from the Big House.

Miss Bond fell in love with Eejay straight away. 'Who is this cute fella, Eddie?' she asked.

'This is Eejay. He's a pure-bred, long-haired Siamese.'

'Wow, pure-bred!' She scooped him up and held him in her arms. 'Where did he come from? He's so beautiful!'

'He was Tilly's cat.' Edward said.

Edward had loved Tilly very much. She was a famous dancer and actress. When they lived at Monkton House she had once left wet footprints on the carpet and Edward had the pattern embroidered into the carpet as a reminder of her. (And that is still there today. Go and see!)

'Well he's divine! I tell you what, let's have a big party and show him off!'

'A party? Well, there is the summer fête at the vicarage...'

'Yes!' Miss Bond pretended to make an announcement: 'CAT COMPETITION AT THE WEST DEAN SUMMER FETE 1935.'

'A cat competition?' Edward said, frowning.

'Yes, but not at the vicarage. Let's have a bigger party at the front of the house. There's more space here and we'll have room for a helter-skelter, donkey rides, fancy dress and Morris dancing!'

'Well, the village would love that.'

'Yes, and we'll invite the Romanies in their painted caravans. We can do a coconut shy... have everyone sitting on bales of hay and dancin' to... Oh! And that new "jazz" music! Can we, Eddie? Please, please, Eddie?'

'Alright, Nancy, we'll have a big party.'

'Oh yes! Promise me, Eddie!'

Edward arranged for posters to be put up in and around West Dean. They read:

113

WEST DEAN
SUMMER FETE
1935

NEW VENUE:
WEST DEAN PARK!

MORRIS DANCERS
FROM THAXTED

THE DUKE ELLINGTON
ORCHESTRA

COMPETITIONS:

TUG OF WAR
BEST TURNIP
BEST VICTORIA SPONGE

BEST CAT

While Mrs Bell was putting one of the posters in the shop window she saw the Woodcutter arrive.

'Mornin', Mrs Bell.'

'Morning, Ted. How's that new kitten of yours?'

'Midnight? Oh, he's a strong 'un now and not so much of a kitten!'

'Growing up quick?'

'Oh yeah! So, your new poster?' he asked, pointing to it.

'Oh! Do you know, I haven't read that myself yet!' She laughed.

'What's this about "Best Cat"?'

'Best Cat?' she repeated.

'Yeah! It says it's one of them competitions!'

'A cat competition? Well, I never! What will they think of next?' Mrs Bell went to the poster to have a look, as she thought of showing everyone Max's tricks.

'Morning, Mrs Bell,' Mr Cooper said, coming through the door.

'Oh, hello!' Ted greeted him. 'Have you heard about the cat competition?'

'The *what* competition?'

'Yes, it's a little bit different, isn't it? I'm not sure if I'll show Spark or Midnight.'

'Well, what do you know? That will be different.' Mr Cooper scratched his head. 'We'll have to give Mabel a proper bath and sort out. You should see her when the Mrs has blow-dried her hair.'

'Blow-dried!?'

Ted had never heard of a blow-dryer and imagined Mrs Cooper energetically blowing all over her cat.

*

News of the summer fête had spread to neighbouring villages, and many people turned up for the event.

Miss Bond had asked the contestants for the cat competition to meet at midday by the cake stall, in the centre of the field near all the attractions. She was dancing by the jazz band when she saw Ben Dunk holding Eejay and waiting for her. She finished her jitterbug and walked with Ben to the cat competition.

Ruby was holding Jaspurr in a basket and he kept on meowing to get out, so Ron stuck his finger through and tickled his chin.

Mr Cat and Mrs Cat were sitting quietly in a pram that Mrs Lyne held firmly to stop it from rolling away. She was talking with Robert and Elsie, who took it in turns to hold Max.

Mabel was on a dog lead, which she really disliked – especially the smell of it.

Miss Pemberton had brought Felicity in the clothes that the children dressed her in at school: a green flamenco dress that matched her eyes.

Ted had brought Midnight. He knew Spark wouldn't enjoy the crowd. He tried to make conversation with Miss Pemberton. She was talking about how amazing it would be to have a wedding breakfast at the Big House. Ted hadn't known that weddings involved breakfast.

The Barn Cat was finishing a hunting expedition by the dovecote when he heard the noise of the fête and followed his nose. It was a little frightening because there were a lot of dogs in the field. There was a pack of foxhounds penned up next to the old Brigadier, who was being Master of the Hounds on his horse. Old Shep's collie was running around freely, ignoring Shep's whistle, and then there was the Manor's Labrador and the Woodcutter's spaniel. But the excitement of it all drew in the Barn Cat. He smelled bacon being fried, and just as he was considering how hot the bacon would be if he jumped up and snatched a bit, he saw lots of cats from the village all grouped together!

When Miss Bond and Ben arrived everyone began talking at the same time.

'Well *someone* has to judge the competition,' said Miss Pemberton. 'It can't be me as I am entering Felicity myself.'

'Yes, quite so, Miss Pemberton, and I can't do it as I have Mr Cat and Mrs Cat here!' Father Harold said.

Everyone turned to Miss Bond.

'Yes! That is a bit difficult, isn't it, and I can't really judge as I am entering Eejay!'

'I can do it, Miss,' Ben Dunk offered.

There was silence followed by muttering from the crowd, but within a few seconds everyone seemed to think that was a good idea.

Ben gently inspected the cats as they sat on a table. Max was the last one to be judged and had started by holding out his paw to shake hands. Mrs Bell collected Max, and Ben concentrated on what his verdict should be. He looked at everyone's faces and knew many would be disappointed, but in that moment the Barn Cat jumped onto the table.

'Oh, sorry, José,' Ben giggled. 'I should have known you'd turn up!'

'Whose cat is that, Ben?' Miss Bond asked, frowning.

'I think it might be Pablo Picasso's.'

Miss Bond knew many famous artists visited the house and so she said nothing.

Ben examined the Barn Cat's paws; they were muddy. He looked at the Barn Cat's teeth; they were more than a little brown. He stroked the Barn Cat's fur and found bits of straw and seeds matted in it. And then there was the old grey hair that the Barn Cat hadn't preened away. He was quite old by now! Finally, Ben felt the bite of a flea that landed on his arm.

'Well, everyone, I've made my decision. First prize goes to José the Barn Cat, and second…'

'I'm sorry, Ben,' Miss Bond interrupted. 'Do you mean the last cat you examined?'

'Yes, Miss Bond.'

'Well… can I ask why, please?' Miss Bond was trying hard to be polite.

'Coz he's done so well, Miss! Livin' outside in the barn through each winter; and, of course, he's the best mouser.'

'Mouser?' Miss Bond repeated.

'He catches lots of mice, Miss!'

'Yeah… I see! But Ben, it's more about being a looker, a pure-bred.'

Father Harold laughed. 'Yes, I would have agreed, Miss Bond. That is the way it's usually done, but hasn't Ben got a point? I think his reasons are admirable!'

The little group of cat owners muttered among themselves and then the Woodcutter declared, 'Midnight must be pure, as he's all black.'

Mrs Cooper said, 'Well Mabel is pure white, and white is more angelic – just like Mabel herself!'

Miss Pemberton also had her say: 'Felicity has got the best costume!'

The Woodcutter said, 'Well if it's all about looks, Miss Bond, I think you should win!'

Ruby declared, 'Jaspurr is the best looker. Look at his boots and bib!'

Mrs Bell said, 'Max should win. He is a working cat and does tricks!'

Each owner was speaking louder and, by the end,

Mrs Bell was shouting. Mr Cooper's dog yapped and he wasn't on his lead as Mabel was wearing it, and then the Woodcutter's dog thought that he should join in the barking too.

The cats didn't like the noise. Mabel jumped free, and the other cats thought that was a good idea and jumped down too.

Ruby was concerned Jaspurr would get trampled, so she raced after him, but in her hurry she accidentally pushed the vicar, who was bending over to pick up Mrs Cat, and he tumbled to the ground. Ruby tried to help Father Harold up but she lost her balance and fell on top of him. Then the barking drew the attention of the foxhounds, who were being taken out of their pen. They thought the barking was more interesting than following the Master on a horse, and they all came over to see what was going on. They ignored the blast of the Master's horn, so he trotted over to gather them up.

Then Old Shep's collie came over to see what the barking was about and joined the Woodcutter's and Mr Cooper's dogs. They all growled at the foxhounds.

Meanwhile, the cats were off! Eejay did an amazing jump up the vicar's back and then sprang from the crown of his head up towards the top of the tent. Sadly, the jump was too ambitious, and Eejay landed on Miss Pemberton instead, who shrieked.

The Master's horse didn't like the kerfuffle and bolted. He jumped the flower stand and the best turnip stand, and then when he saw Mabel in the grass he stopped suddenly and headed back from whence he'd come. In the sharp turn the old Brigadier came off the horse and landed next to Mabel, who licked his nose.

The horse jumped back over the best turnip stand, but when he saw all the cats running around he changed direction and headed for the beer tent, scattering the Morris dancers. The table with all the cakes was in his way! He managed a good jump but just caught the first prize Victoria sponge; it splattered all over Ruby and the vicar, who were both still trying to get up off the ground.

This was the Barn Cat's prize, and he sat down in the middle of the vicar's hat and tucked into the fresh cream of the cake.

The Woodcutter raced after Midnight, who had run almost as far as the woods.

'Midnight, it's Dad. You're alright.' Midnight meowed his appreciation and was placed in the pocket of the Woodcutter's wax jacket, which was quite a squeeze now Midnight had grown.

Mrs Cooper found Mabel under the cake table finishing off a vanilla slice.

Felicity and Eejay shared a few moments together on the top of the tent, looking down on the chaos.

Max was carried home by both Robert and Elsie, as they couldn't remember whose turn it was.

Mrs Lyne had returned Mr Cat and Mrs Cat to the pram and put Jaspurr in there too while the vicar and Ruby wiped off the cream, jam and mud from their faces.

I think we should leave them all now while they sort themselves out. I hope you enjoyed the village fête and hope to see you back here next year.

One last thing before I go: I hope you try and visit West Dean, and if you bump into a cat there or anywhere else, practise speaking cat. It only takes a slow blink and a tickle under the chin.

About the Author

Luke McEwen, the second son of Andrew and Anitra McEwen, was born in Chichester, West Sussex, in 1964. Andrew, a journalist for the Daily Mail for 26 years, was chief diplomatic correspondent for the Times in the latter years of his career. Luke spent four years of his childhood in Freeport, New York, and 18 months in Brussels, where he attended the Common Market School, before finally returning to his home town nine years later in 1973.

Luke studied Politics and Sociology at the University of East Anglia although, sadly, he did not attend the UEA's famous writing course. He did, however, attend the creative writing course at Chichester College led by Julia Homan.

Luke is a keen potter and painter and enjoys playing tennis and the saxophone. He continues to work and live in Chichester with his son.

Luke is the author of the novel *Films and Fathers* and an anthology of adult short stories entitled *One Last Cruise*.

Luke's blog and writers' website can be found at www.lukemcewen.co.uk.

A Bit More About Ben Dunk

Hello, I'm Ben Dunk, the judge from the cat competition. What an imagination Luke has! He asked me if he could use me as a character in his cat stories, and of course I said yes. I loved the idea of celebrating the relationship between man and his cat. I'll let you decide if the stories ever really happened, but if you'd like to hear more about my childhood in West Dean and what actually did happen during that time then please read all about it at http://www.dunkantix.com/Secrets.

Here is a photograph of me with my parents. My dad, Charles Alfred Dunk, is dressed up 'dandyish', ready to go to a whist drive in the local school, ending up with a social drink at The Selsey Arms. There's me in the middle. It was my fourth birthday. And on the right, my mother, Ada Florence Jane Dunk (née Stickland). She is holding Sally, the Jack Russell terrier, a fearless dog who liked to chase the farm cats – or any other animal, for that matter.

When I was a boy there were no other children in West Dean Park for me to make friends with. I was the only child in that house from 1929 to 1944. But that didn't stop me having fun and adventures. I made West Dean Estate my own and knew most of the people there. I even saw the king!

I remember those days as if they were yesterday: the wonderful people and the days when things were simpler and there was more time for ourselves. Now that I am nearly 90 years old I look back with a lifetime of beautiful memories and I urge you, if you ever get the chance, to visit West Dean for yourself. Go and make your own adventure.

*

… One final picture of me and my pals at Home Farm. Here I am seated on millstone, and hence my theory that there was once a water-driven flour mill on the site of Home Farm. There were other stone relics, built into the adjacent cottages. I believe that I am about 4 years old in the picture… 1934-ish!! The Jack Russell terrier is Sally and the big grey fluffy cat is Aloysius, owned by Miss Roberts, our neighbour. This cat spent a lot of its time with me, in our garden. Incidentally, the dog and cat were great friends.

Printed in Great Britain
by Amazon